I Like to Read® books, created by award-winning picture book artists as well as talented newcomers, instill confidence and the joy of reading in new readers.

We want to hear every new reader say, "I like to read!"

I Like My Bike

AG Ferrari

I Like to Read®

HOLIDAY HOUSE • NEW YORK

Library of Congress Cataloging-in-Publication Data
Names: Ferrari, Antongionata, 1960– author, illustrator.
Title: I like my bike / AntonGionata Ferrari.
Description: First edition. | New York : Holiday House, [2019] Series:
I like to read | Summary: Illustrations and easy-to-read text show the advantages
of being on a bicycle when streets are jammed with other vehicles.
Identifiers: LCCN 2018001427| ISBN 9780823440979 (hardcover)
ISBN 9780823440986 (pbk.)
Subjects: | CYAC: Bicycles and bicycling—Fiction. | Traffic
congestion—Fiction. | Motor vehicles—Fiction.
Classification: LCC PZ7.1.F466 Iaam 2019 | DDC [E]—dc23 LC record
available at https://lccn.loc.gov/2018001427

ISBN 978-0-8234-4097-9 (hardcover)

To Tiziana,
who loves cycling

I like my bike.

I like my car.

I like my car.

I like my van.

I like my bus.

I like my truck.

I like my truck.

I like my truck.

I like my bike.